GW00857900

The Easter Bunny's Missing Basket

KATHLEEN B. MURPHY

Lovingly restored by Michele Murphy Gastel

RED PENGUIN Books

The Easter Bunny's Missing Basket
Copyright © 2021 by Kathleen B. Murphy
All rights reserved
Published by Red Penguin Books
Bellerose Village, New York
Library of Congress Control Number:2021913708
ISBN
Softcover 978-1-63777-112-9
Hardcover 978-1-63777-129-7
Digital 978-1-63777-113-6

No part of this book may be reproduced in any form
or by any electronic or mechanical means, including
information storage and retrieval systems, without
written permission from the author, except for the
use of brief quotations in a book review.

*It is a joy for me to dedicate this book to
my third grade teacher, Miss Florence Tromer,
who later became Mrs. Florence Campbell.
She was my all-time favorite teacher
and my role model as I undertook the journey
of becoming a teacher.*

*I also must acknowledge my professors
at Fordham University's Undergraduate
School of Education, especially the one
who required us to write a story for
elementary education students!*

Thank you all!

It was getting close
to Easter,
and the Easter Bunny
could not find his
basket full of eggs.

He looked and looked but he could not find it in his messy room.

"Maybe I lost it somewhere in this big city," he said.
"I must find it, or there will be no Easter!"

He looked on the subway, but it was not there.

He took a ride on the ferry boat, but he could not find the basket.

The Statue of Liberty was very nice, but she had not seen it.

He looked in the Empire State Building from top to bottom, but it was not there.

He looked all
around the
U.N. Building,
but it was not
there either.

Next he went to the Bronx Zoo. He asked the lion about the basket, but the lion just yawned and said, "I don't have it."

The giraffe was very nice to the Easter Bunny.
He said, "I'll look way up here in the trees for your basket." But it was not there either.

Then he looked in the monkey's cage, but they did not have it.

He left the zoo
and looked in all
the tunnels ...

... and on
all the
bridges.

But he simply

could not find it!

Now the Easter Bunny was so tired and so sad, he just sat down and cried.

As he walked home he was very unhappy. "If I don't find my basket, there will be no Easter!" he said.

His mother was waiting for him at the door. She found his basket! She found it at the bottom of his very messy closet!

The Easter Bunny was very happy.
Now there could be an Easter!
And ever since that day, he has kept his room very neat and clean!

About The Author

Kathleen Murphy is a retired NYC teacher and administrator who wrote this story in her senior of college. It has long-been on her "bucket list" to get it published so that many more parents and grandparents get to share it with their little ones.

Lightning Source UK Ltd.
Milton Keynes UK
UKRC011318230821
389119UK00002B/9